Four & Twenty
Dinosaurs

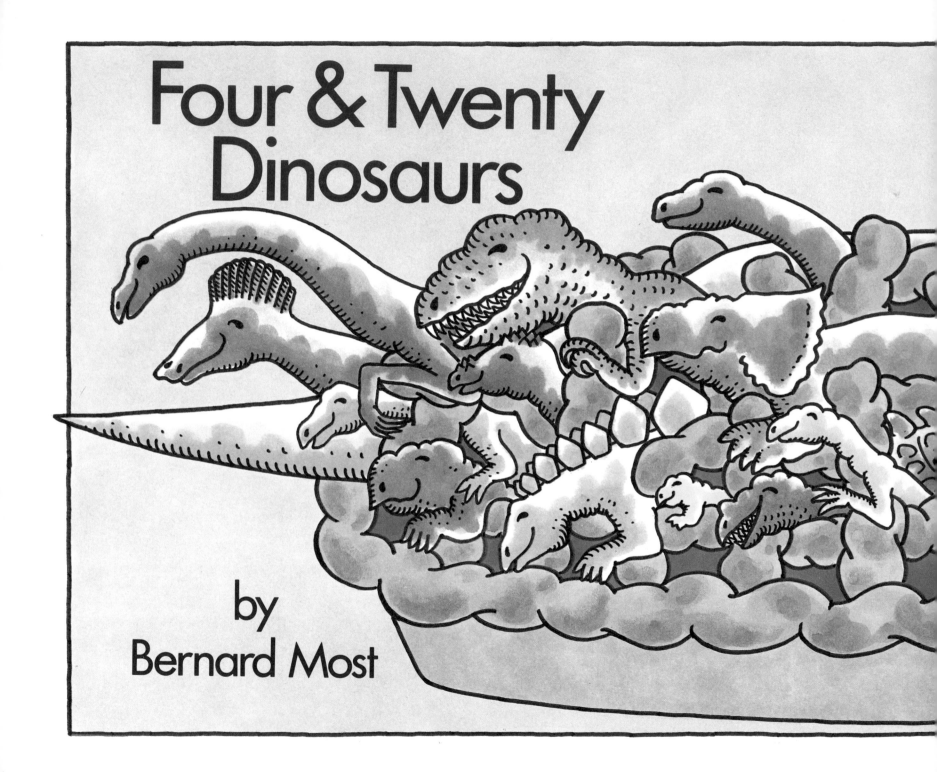

Four & Twenty Dinosaurs

by
Bernard Most

Harper & Row, Publishers

To the High School of Art and Design in New York City

Four & Twenty Dinosaurs
Copyright © 1990 by Bernard Most
Printed in the U.S.A. All rights reserved.
1 2 3 4 5 6 7 8 9 10
First Edition

Library of Congress Cataloging-in-Publication Data
Most, Bernard.
  Four & twenty dinosaurs / by Bernard Most.
      p.   cm.
  Summary: Dinosaurs are substituted for the main characters in this
illustrated collection of traditional nursery rhymes.
  ISBN 0-06-024376-7 : $. — ISBN 0-06-024377-5 (lib. bdg.) : $
  1. Nursery rhymes. 2. Children's poetry.   [1. Nursery rhymes.
2. Dinosaurs—Poetry.] I. Title.
PZ8.3.M847Fo 1990   89-34472
398.8—dc20   CIP
                                                                   AC

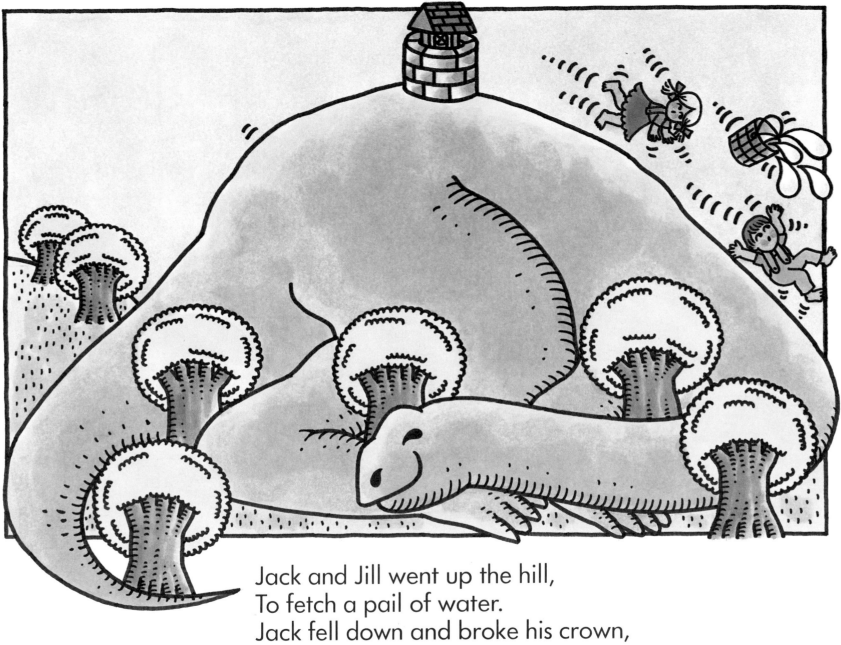

Jack and Jill went up the hill,
To fetch a pail of water.
Jack fell down and broke his crown,
And Jill came tumbling after.
Said Jack to Jill, "That was no hill!
That was a Brontosaurus."

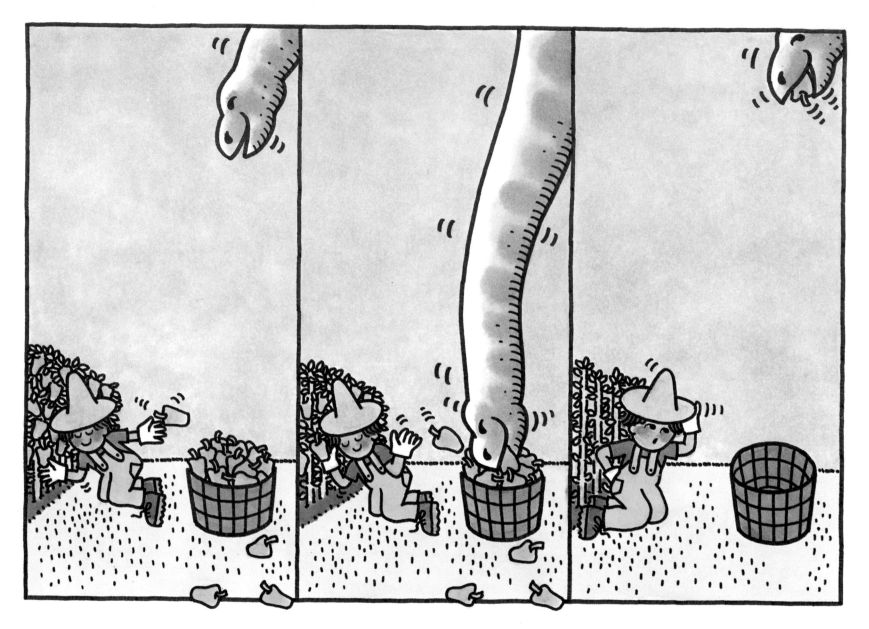

Peter Piper picked a peck of pickled peppers;
A peck of pickled peppers Peter Piper picked.
If Peter Piper picked a peck of pickled peppers,
Where's the peck of pickled peppers Peter Piper picked?

Rain on the green grass,
And rain on the tree,
Rain on the housetop,
But not on me.

Hark! Hark! The dogs do bark,
The dinosaurs are coming to town;
Some in rags and some in Jags,
And one in a velvet gown.

Pat-a-cake, pat-a-cake, baker's man,
Bake me a cake as fast as you can,
Pat it, and prick it, and mark it with a "B,"
Put it in the oven for Bactrosaurus and me.

Needles and pins,
Needles and pins,
When dinosaurs marry,
Their trouble begins.

London Bridge is falling down,
Falling down, falling down,
London Bridge is falling down,
My fair lady!

Build it up with iron and steel,
Iron and steel, iron and steel,
Build it up with iron and steel,
My fair lady!

Diddle, diddle, dumpling, my Iguanodon
Went to bed with his trousers on.
One shoe off, and one shoe on,
Diddle, diddle, dumpling, my Iguanodon.

"Bow-wow," say the dogs,
"Meow-meow," say the cats,
"Grunt-grunt," go the hogs,
And "squeak," go the rats.

"Caw-caw," say the crows,
"Quack-quack," say the ducks,
What did the dinosaurs say?
Nobody knows.

Little Miss Muffet sat on her tuffet,
Eating her curds and whey;
Along came a spider,
And sat down beside her.
Did it frighten Miss Muffet away?

Go to bed late,
Stay very small.
Go to bed early,
Grow very tall.

Higher than a house,
Higher than a tree,
Oh, whatever can that be?

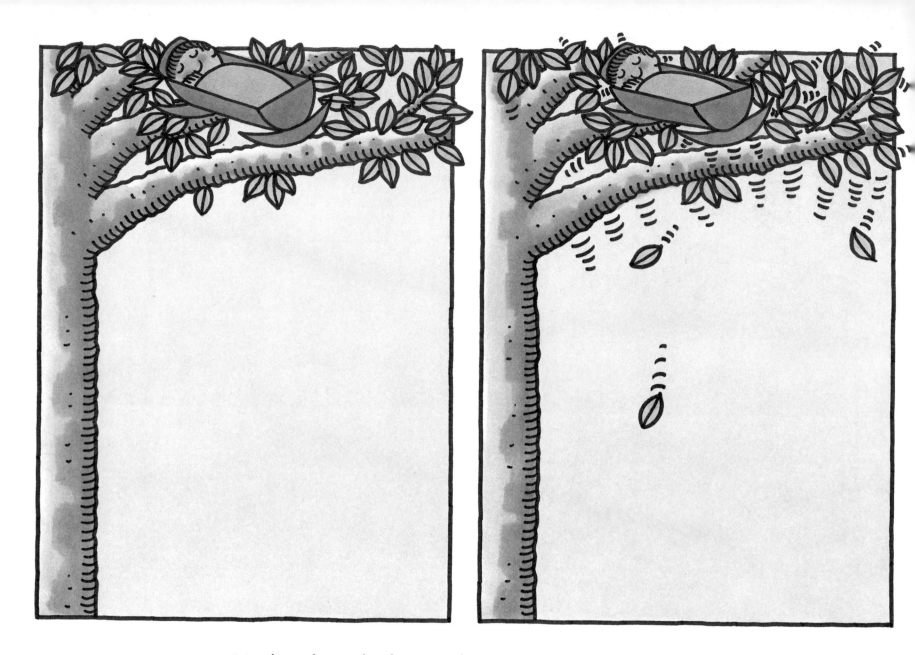

Hush-a-bye, baby, in the treetop,
When the wind blows, the cradle will rock,
When the bough breaks, the cradle will fall,
Down will come baby, cradle and all.

Little Jack Horner sat in a corner,
Eating a Christmas pie;
He put in his thumb, and pulled out a plum,
And said, "What a good Protoceratops am I!"

Here we go round the mulberry bush,
The mulberry bush, the mulberry bush,
Here we go round the mulberry bush,
On a cold and frosty morning.

One, two, three, four and five,
I caught an Allosaurus alive!
Six, seven, eight, nine and ten,
I let it go again.

Why did you let it go?
Because it bit my finger so!
Which finger did it bite?
The little finger on the right.

Old Mother Hubbard
Went to the cupboard,
To fetch her poor dog a bone.

But when she got there,
The cupboard was bare,
And so her poor dog had none.

Hey diddle, diddle,
Where's the cat and the fiddle?
Where's the cow that jumped over the moon?
Where's the little dog that laughed to see such sport?
Where's the dish that ran away with the spoon?

Cobbler, cobbler, mend my shoe,
Get it done by half past two.
Stitch it up, and stitch it down,
Then I'll give you half a crown.

Mary had a little Lambeosaurus,
With feet as white as snow.
And everywhere that Mary went,
The Lambeosaurus was sure to go.

It followed her to school one day,
Which was against the rule.
It made the children laugh and play,
To see a Lambeosaurus at school.

Sing a song of sixpence,
A pocketful of rye;
Four and twenty dinosaurs,
Baked in a pie.

When the pie was opened,
They all began to sing;
Was that not a dainty dish,
To set before the king?

Three little kittens,
They lost their mittens,
And they began to cry,
Oh mother dear, we sadly fear,
Our mittens we have lost.

What! lost your mittens,
You naughty kittens!
Then you shall have no pie.
Mee-ow, mee-ow, mee-ow,
No, you shall have no pie.

There was an old woman who lived in a shoe.
She had so many Triceratopses, she didn't know what to do.
She gave them some broth, without any bread,
She spanked them all soundly and sent them to bed.

The man in the moon,
Looked out of the moon,
Looked out of the moon and said:
"'Tis time for all Tyrannosauruses on earth,
To think about getting to bed!"